LITTLE MISS BAD

Roger Hargreaves

D0489015

Written and illustrated by
Adam Hargreaves

Little Miss Sunshine looked out of the window and thought back on all the things that had happened in the last week.

Lots of things.

Lots of bad things.

Some things were just a little bit bad.

Mr Uppity's tennis racquet strings were swapped for spaghetti.

And the cream in Mr Greedy's cream buns was replaced with toothpaste.

Some things were really quite bad.

Little Miss Splendid's shower had covered her with ink.

And someone had painted cracks on the walls of Mr Worry's house.

Mr Worry was so worried that his house might fall down, he had moved into his garden shed.

Some things were really very bad indeed!

Someone had sawn Mr Forgetful's car in half.
Fortunately, Mr Forgetful did not get upset.
He simply thought that he must have forgotten the
other half and left it at home.

And someone had sneaked into Little Miss Neat's house while she was away on holiday and left all the taps running.

Little Miss Neat did get upset.

Nobody knew who had done all these things, but Little Miss Sunshine had a very good idea who was behind it all.

"Little Miss Bad," she murmured to herself.

Little Miss Bad was not good.

Far from it.

In fact, about as far as you can get, which is a long way.

But how to catch Little Miss Bad? This was the question that Little Miss Sunshine was turning over in her mind.

And then she had an idea.

A very clever idea.

The next day a poster appeared in the Town Square. It announced that there was to be a 'Grand Competition' to discover the most mischievous, naughty or bad trick that had been played in the last week. First prize was a fabulous holiday.

"How easy," said Little Miss Bad to herself.
"That holiday is as good as mine."

The day of the Grand Competition dawned.
By midday a large crowd had gathered in the Town Square. A stage had been built in the middle of the square.

Little Miss Sunshine called for quiet.

"Each contestant," she explained, "will come up on stage and describe their entry and then the panel of judges will decide upon a winner. First up is Little Miss Bad!"

Little Miss Bad could not wait to get on stage.

She was so excited.

She had spent all the previous night trying to pick her worst or best trick, depending on how you looked at it, but she had not been able to decide.

So she described them all to the crowd. From Mr Uppity's tennis racquet strings all the way through to Little Miss Neat's wet house.

She described them in great detail.

Little Miss Bad was so carried away she failed to notice that the crowd had fallen silent. It was only when she had finished that she saw the expressions on everyone's faces.

She looked to Little Miss Sunshine, who was the only person in the square with a smile on her face, a rather smug smile, and it suddenly occurred to Little Miss Bad just what she had been tricked into doing.

"I-I-I was only j-j-joking," she stammered.

"Anything more to say?" said Little Miss Sunshine.

Little Miss Bad looked very ashamed. "I'm sorry," she said.

Little Miss Bad had learnt her lesson that day.

The lesson continued for a number of weeks as it took her a long time to repair all the damage and clean Little Miss Neat's house.

Mr Forgetful's car will never look quite the same. Luckily he can't remember what it looked like in the first place.

But nothing she had to do was half as bad as those moments standing on the stage with the crowd glaring at her.

It was a very long time before she even thought of doing anything bad.

And the same could be said of one other person that day.

Mr Mischief.

Who slipped away from his place next to the stage and slunk off home, where he breathed a very deep sigh of relief!

Fantastic offers for Little Miss fans!

Collect all your Mr. Men or Little Miss books in these superb durable collectors' cases!

Only £5.99 inc. postage and packing, these wipe-clean, hard-wearing cases will give all your Mr. Men or Little Miss books a beautiful new home!

Keep track of your collection with this giant-sized double-sided Mr. Men and Little Miss Collectors' poster.

Collect 6 tokens and we will send you a brilliant giant-sized double-sided collectors' poster! Simply tape a £1 coin to cover postage and packaging in the space provided and fill out the form overleaf.

STICK £1 COIN HERE (for poster only)

Only need a few Little Miss or Mr. Men to complete your set? You can order any of the titles on the back of the books from our Mr. Men order line on 0870 787 1724. Orders should be delivered between 5 and 7 working days.

— **TO BE COMPLETED BY AN ADULT** —

To apply for any of these great offers, ask an adult to complete the details below and send this whole page with the appropriate payment and tokens, to: MR. MEN CLASSIC OFFER, PO BOX 715, HORSHAM RH12 5WG

☐ Please send me a giant-sized double-sided collectors' poster.
AND ☐ I enclose 6 tokens and have taped a £1 coin to the other side of this page.

☐ Please send me ☐ Mr. Men Library case(s) and/or ☐ Little Miss library case(s) at £5.99 each inc P&P

☐ I enclose a cheque/postal order payable to Egmont UK Limited for £............

OR ☐ Please debit my MasterCard / Visa / Maestro / Delta account (delete as appropriate) for £............

Card no. ☐☐☐☐☐☐☐☐☐☐☐☐☐☐☐☐☐☐☐ Security code ☐☐☐

Issue no. (if available) ☐ Start Date ☐☐/☐☐/☐☐ Expiry Date ☐☐/☐☐/☐☐

Fan's name: .... Date of birth: ....

Address: ....

....

Postcode: ....

Name of parent / guardian: ....

Email for parent / guardian: ....

Signature of parent / guardian: ....

Please allow 28 days for delivery. Offer is only available while stocks last. We reserve the right to change the terms of this offer at any time and we offer a 14 day money back guarantee. This does not affect your statutory rights. Offers apply to UK only.

☐ We may occasionally wish to send you information about other Egmont children's books.
If you would rather we didn't, please tick this box.

Ref: LIM 001